DATE			

DEMCO

The
GINGERBREAD
BOY

RICHARD EGIELSKI

A LAURA GERINGER BOOK
An Imprint of HarperCollinsPublishers

The Gingerbread Boy
Copyright © 1997 by Richard Egielski
Printed in the U.S.A. All rights reserved.

Library of Congress Cataloging-in-Publication Data
Egielski, Richard.
  The gingerbread boy / Richard Egielski.
     p.   cm.
  "A Laura Geringer book."
  Summary: A freshly baked gingerbread boy escapes when he is taken
out of the oven and eludes his pursuers until he meets a clever fox.
  ISBN 0-06-026030-0.
  [1. Fairy tales. 2. Folklore.] I. Gingerbread boy. II. Title.
PZ8.E289Gi 1997   95-50026
[E]   CIP
                                                         AC

Typography by Alicia Mikles
2 3 4 5 6 7 8 9 10
❖

For Sheldon Fogelman

There was a woman and a man who had no children.

One day the woman took flour, eggs, butter, brown sugar, molasses, ginger, cinnamon, salt, a pinch of black pepper and made some dough. She rolled it flat and cut out the shape of a little boy. Then with candy, nuts, and icing, she made his face and clothes.

"There you are," she said, "my Gingerbread Boy!" And she put him in the oven to bake.

He baked up nice and brown but so hot that he shot right out of the oven, across the room, and through the open window.

The woman and the man cried, "Gingerbread Boy, please stop!"

But the Gingerbread Boy only laughed and said, "Run run run as fast as you can. You can't catch me! I'm the Gingerbread Man."

And off he ran.

Until he met a rat.

"You smell good," said the rat. "I'm going to eat you!"

But the Gingerbread Boy only laughed and said, "Run run run as fast as you can. You can't catch me! I'm the Gingerbread Man."

And off he ran.

Until he met some construction workers.

"Hey you! Gingerbread Boy!" they shouted.

"You're just the snack for our coffee break!"

But the Gingerbread Boy only laughed and said, "Run run run as fast as you can. You can't catch me! I'm the Gingerbread Man."

And off he ran.

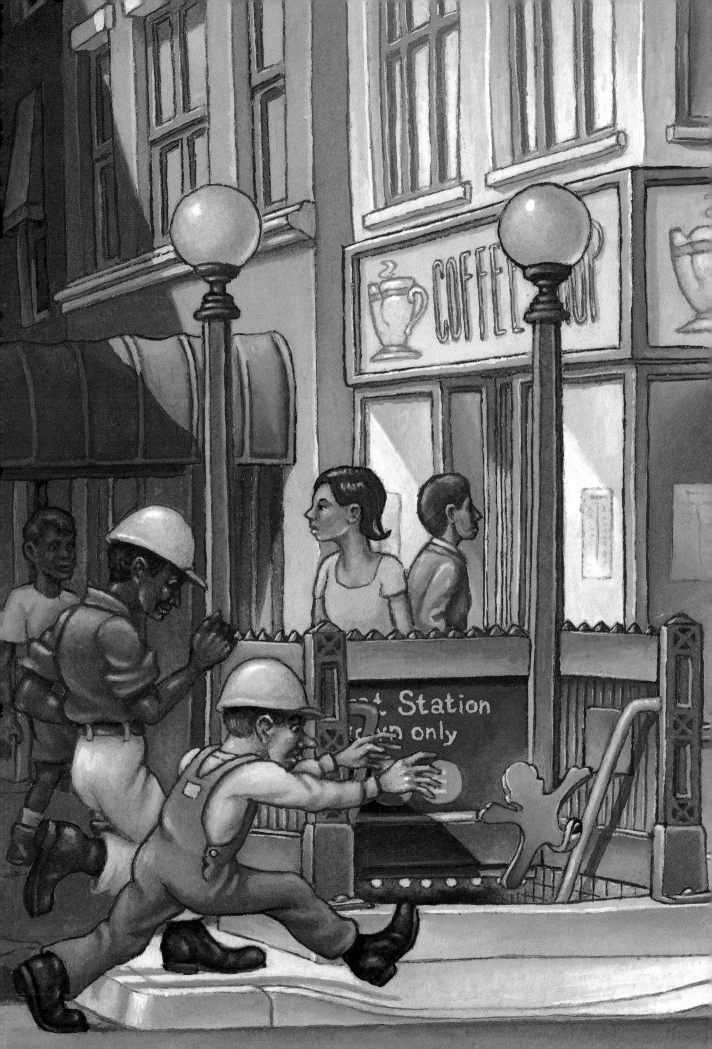

Until he met some musicians.

"Yummy! Yummy! Yummy!" they sang.

But the Gingerbread Boy only laughed and said, "Run run run as fast as you can. You can't catch me! I'm the Gingerbread Man."

And off he ran.

Until he met a policeman on a horse. "Stop! Stop in the name of the law!" the policeman called. "We're hungry!"

But the Gingerbread Boy only laughed and said, "Run run run as fast as you can. You can't catch me! I'm the Gingerbread Man."

And off he ran.

Until he met a fox.

By now the Gingerbread Boy was feeling pretty proud of himself.

"I've run away from the woman and the man, the rat, the construction workers, the musicians, and the policeman on a horse—and I can run away from you too!" he bragged. "Run run run . . ."

"No! No! No!" the fox interrupted. "I don't want to eat you. But there is a big lake up ahead. And that crowd you're running from is catching up."

"Oh! What shall I do?" asked the Gingerbread Boy.

"Hop onto my tail, and I'll carry you across!" said the fox. So the Gingerbread Boy hopped onto the fox's tail.

Then the fox said, "It will be easier to hold on if you climb onto my shoulders."

So the Gingerbread Boy climbed onto the fox's shoulders.

"This lake is deeper than I thought," said the fox, "and if you get wet, you'll crumble away to nothing. Why don't you crawl out onto my nose?"

So the Gingerbread Boy crawled out onto the fox's nose.

"Ha! Ha!" laughed the Gingerbread Boy. "They'll never get me now!"

"You're right," said the fox as she flipped him into the air. And she opened her mouth . . .

and the Gingerbread Boy was all gone.